DATE DUE   EG   5/07

JUN 2 5 2007					
JUL 0 5 2007					
JUL 0 5 2007					
AUG 1 1 2007					
AUG 1 7 2007					

DEMCO, INC. 38-3011

OSCAR WILDE'S

THE HAPPY PRINCE

AS RETOLD BY ELISSA GRODIN

ILLUSTRATED BY LAURA STUTZMAN

To my editor, Barbara McNally

ELISSA

For Mark

LAURA

*The illustrator would like to thank the people who gave their time
and patience to this project and make working from "life" possible.*

Derek Upperman as "The Happy Prince"

*And in order of appearance: Donna & Bill Aspinall, Darlene Terlizzi, Ivan Stutzman, Mark Stutzman, Arlene Murray,
Judy Devlin, Rob Michael, Austin Eyler, Christy Eyler, Katie Eyler, Corey Lewis, Bailey Michael, Elizabeth Thayer,
Amber Upperman, The Republican Newspaper Players, Barbara Michael, Emmett Michael, John Zimmerman,
Theodore Ringer III, Kenzie McCauley, Trevor Kroll, Nikki Stalnaker, Sheri Sisler, Keshawn Rhodes, Korey Mitchum,
Haley Mitchum, Olivia Mitchum, Crockett, Ann & Clint Englander & Brocca, Falon Stutzman & Tula.*

For their expertise: Melodie Hill (costumer), Little Yough Chocolates, Streams & Dreams, and Crellin Elementary School.

Text Copyright © 2006 Elissa Grodin
Illustration Copyright © 2006 Laura Stutzman

Sleeping Bear Press™

310 North Main Street, Suite 300
Chelsea, MI 48118
www.sleepingbearpress.com

THOMSON
✳
GALE

© 2006 Thomson Gale, a part of the Thomson Corporation.
Thomson, Star Logo and Sleeping Bear Press are trademarks
and Gale is a registered trademark used herein under license.

Printed and bound in Canada.

First Edition

10 9 8 7 6 5 4 3 2 1

Grodin, Elissa, 1954-
The happy prince / retold by Elissa Grodin ; illustrated by Laura Stutzman.
p. cm.
Summary: A beautiful, golden, jewel-studded statue and a little
swallow give all they have to help the poor.
ISBN 1-58536-264-6
[1. Fairy tales.] I. Stutzman, Laura, ill. II. Wilde, Oscar, 1854-1900.
Happy prince. III. Title.
PZ8.G8885Hap 2006
[E]—dc22
2006001867

OSCAR WILDE

OSCAR FINGAL O'FLAHERTIE WILLS WILDE was born on October 16, 1854, in Dublin, Ireland. He had an older brother, Willie, and a younger sister, Isola. Oscar Wilde lived in Victorian times, which means during the reign of Queen Victoria, which lasted from 1837 to 1901.

Mr. Wilde wrote poetry, plays, reviews, short stories, fairy tales, and one novel. His comedic plays, which poke fun at society, are still being produced around the world. They include *The Importance of Being Earnest, Lady Windermere's Fan, An Ideal Husband*, and others. His only novel, *The Picture of Dorian Gray*, a supernatural tale about a man who never grows old, was based on *The Strange Case of Dr. Jekyll and Mr. Hyde*, by R. L. Stevenson.

Mr. Wilde openly borrowed ideas from other writers, but the imprint of his own personality and talent on his material was so great that he enjoyed terrific success, particularly as a playwright. He is considered to be a very distinguished writer to this day.

When Mr. Wilde had two sons of his own, it is likely that he felt inspired to write fairy tales. His stories were influenced by the tales of Hans Christian Andersen. Because Mr. Wilde was an outspoken and opinionated thinker, his fairy tales contain serious ideas about how he thought people should behave in society. He intended his fairy tales for adults as well as children. In fact, the majority of these stories are dedicated to adult friends.

While visiting some students at Cambridge University, Mr. Wilde came up with the idea for "The Happy Prince." The students enjoyed hearing his story so much that Mr. Wilde wrote it down as soon as he got back to his room. *The Happy Prince and Other Tales* was published in 1888.

Oscar Wilde died on November 30, 1900.

It HAD BEEN SEVERAL weeks since the rest of the swallows had flown south for the winter. Little Swallow didn't care. The trees still had most of their leaves, and he was having fun swooping through the woods at the river's edge, with the place all to himself. The sun warmed his body as he splashed among the wildflowers and reeds along the riverbank. They murmured admiringly at his glistening feathers and lustrous eyes. Swallow pretended not to hear.

By and by, as the sun set earlier each evening, the days grew shorter and shorter. The wildflowers faded to brown and were no longer beautiful. The reeds stiffened and turned silent. The chilly wind ruffled the Swallow's feathers. It was time for him to set off and join the rest of his flock.

He flew for many hours, and decided to stop overnight in the Great City to rest.

Swallow circled high above the dreary-looking city, keeping an eye out for a suitable place to roost for the night.

After a bit, he spied a patch of green. Swooping down for closer inspection, Swallow discovered a beautiful little park. It looked as if no one had ever used it, and indeed, there was a forbidding fence all around. No sooner had Swallow landed on the branch of an old oak tree than a group of people, including the mayor, approached.

"This, good visitors, is our fair city's pride and joy," the mayor said grandly. The distinguished group looked up admiringly at a gold-covered, jewel-encrusted statue standing high atop a tall column.

"This statue is known as the Happy Prince," the mayor intoned, "for during his lifetime, the prince was the finest of men. He lived all his years inside the royal palace, enjoying the best foods, the best jugglers, musicians, and dancers, and the loyal company of hundreds of friends. He was not only the happiest of men, but also the handsomest. Isn't this the most beautiful statue you've ever seen?"

The mayor stepped back to gaze at the statue's magnificent rubies, emeralds, sapphires, and gold.

"The Happy Prince is very beautiful, indeed," murmured the visitors. "Your city is all the more lovely because of it."

"Yes, indeed," said the mayor. "You can see he has the highest place of honor here. This park is kept in perfect condition and no one is allowed to play here. Nothing is allowed to spoil this beautiful setting."

The Swallow observed all this from his perch in the tree. When the mayor and his group had moved along, Swallow decided the statue would make a good roost for the night.

As the moon rose in the sky, the little bird settled in between the Prince's feet, where he would be sheltered from the wind and the elements. Just as he was drifting off to sleep, a large drop of water fell on his head. The bird brushed it off and buried his head deeper under his wing. After a few moments another drop fell on his head. Protected by the statue, the Swallow could not understand why he was getting wet from the rain. He looked up.

To his amazement, he saw that the eyes of the Happy Prince were filled with tears! The moonlight shone brightly on the handsome, golden face, now streaming with tears.

Astonished, Swallow asked, "What's the matter? Why are you crying?"

The Prince looked down at the little bird.

"You heard my story. I lived a very happy life at the palace. I had everything I wanted there, and I never ventured out. Now that I am a statue I can see high above the palace walls. I can see everything in the city. I never knew the world had such sadness in it. Every day and every night I see the struggles and hardships so many people face. Their lives are so different from the life I had. And standing here on this pedestal, I can do nothing to help them."

Swallow thought about it and asked, "But what could you do, anyway?"

"Come here and sit on my shoulder," the Prince said. "Now, look past the clock tower to the cathedral. Do you see that little gray house just beyond it? Look hard and you can see a woman inside and some little children. The woman is sad because even though she tries her best and works so hard, she will soon lose her house because she cannot pay the bills. I want you to take the ruby from my crown and give it to her. She needs it more than I do. When she sells it, she will have enough money to pay her bills."

"Oh," said the Swallow. "I don't really think *I* can help. I'm so tired and have flown a long, long way and still have farther to travel. I must get some sleep because my friends are waiting for me."

The Prince smiled at the little bird. "Have you ever felt cold and needed a place to sleep?" the Prince asked.

"I don't know—I guess so," Swallow answered.

"When I lived in my palace," said the Prince, "I never worried about the rain or the cold. The palace was large and comfortable and had more rooms than I needed."

Soaking wet from the Prince's tears, the little bird was tired and did not want to fly anywhere. "All right, just this once," he grumbled. "But then I must get some sleep."

The Swallow plucked the ruby from the center of the Prince's crown. He flew across the city, over rooftops and along narrow streets. He found the shabby gray house and flew in through the kitchen window. He placed the jewel on the wooden table.

When the woman discovered the ruby she was overcome with joy.
Tears ran down her face. Laughing and crying at the same time,
she kissed her children and hugged them close to her.

When the Swallow returned to the Prince, he told him
what had happened and how happy the woman was.
The little bird was so exhausted from all the commotion
that he soon fell asleep. He dreamed that night about
happy children tucked into cozy beds inside rooms
with warm fires crackling in the fireplaces.

THE NEXT MORNING Swallow woke up refreshed and was getting ready to leave when the Prince spoke.

"Good morning," he said. "I hope you slept well."

"Yes, indeed I did," said the Swallow. "I dreamt about happy children snuggled up in cozy beds."

"It is a beautiful, crisp day. Why don't you spend it with me?" said the Prince, smiling a sad sort of smile. "I can tell you more about my city."

Swallow thought about his friends splashing in the warm lakes to the south. He felt annoyed by the Prince's request. But the Prince looked rather pitiful with a big hole in his crown where the ruby used to be, and the bird felt bad for him.

"I suppose the flock will wait for me," he chirped. "I will stay with you for a day."

The day went by quickly as the Prince told stories of his life in the palace. The little bird listened, mesmerized by accounts of strange and marvelous visitors from faraway lands. He especially enjoyed the Prince's descriptions of the exotic and wonderful foods that the palace cook used to prepare. Swallow daydreamed about buttered cardoons and gooseberry cake.

"You know, Swallow, it's a terrible thing to go hungry, and yet every day I see people without enough to eat. In fact, there is a group of poor people who live under the bridge. They exist on scraps of food left behind by others, but they will starve to death in the winter if they do not have more to eat."

The little bird listened thoughtfully as the Prince continued.

"I am covered in gold. Peel it off leaf by leaf and distribute it among the bridge people. With it, they will be able to buy food for the winter."

Swallow did not think the Prince should strip himself of his beautiful golden covering, but the Prince had made up his mind. The bird gently pulled off the gold, leaf by leaf.

Without his gold covering the Prince looked gray and lifeless. Swallow didn't mention it, though. He didn't want to hurt his friend's feelings.

Clutched in the bird's beak, the gold leaves were awkward and
heavy to carry. Swallow's wings ached by the time he reached
the bridge people.

Standing under the bridge, they huddled around a fire.
Their eyes were dull from hardship and they shivered
in the chilly night air.

Swallow flew overhead and slowly released the gold leaves one by one. The people looked up in amazement. As they realized what was happening, they jumped up to snatch the bits of gold, and danced with glee.

Back at the park, the Prince listened quietly as the Swallow told him about the bridge people. When the bird had finished the Prince said, "You have done a fine job, my little friend." Swallow smiled proudly, his small chest puffing up with a happy heart.

And so it went on for several days. Each morning the Happy Prince looked out across the Great City, where he could see into all its corners. He sent the Swallow where help was needed, and soon enough, all the jewels from his crown and sword were gone.

"Finished at last," said Swallow, feeling rather pleased with himself.

"THERE IS ONE LAST thing to be done," the Prince said gently. "There is an old school at the edge of town. The children there are sad and bored, for the school has no money for books or colored paper, nor for crayons and pencils."

"Swallow," he continued, "pry the sapphires from my eyes and take them to the schoolhouse. With the sapphires the teacher can buy books and paints to excite the children's minds, and games and pets to warm their hearts."

"But Prince," Swallow cried, "you will be blind!"

"Ah, but the children have a greater need. I will manage all right."

The Swallow felt a terrible lump in his throat. He started to cry, but quickly brushed the tears away with his wing.

"I will do it," the little bird said, his voice cracking slightly.

So Swallow gently pecked loose the sapphires and clamped them in his beak.

The weather had gotten colder and a frosty wind stung the Swallow's eyes as he flew across the Great City. He soared out over the swirling spires and towers, and swooped down across the trees at the edge of the city.

The schoolhouse was a drab brick building with only a small strip of stubby grass for a playground. Finding a hole in the roof, Swallow flew in.

The children perked up and smiled when they saw him circling the room. The teacher started to chase him out with a broom until the Swallow dropped the sapphires. The children leapt up from their seats, laughing and clapping.

By the time the Swallow returned to the Prince, the tips of his wings had frost on them. He flapped his wings hard and tried to warm himself up.

"I am back, my Prince," the little bird said. "And something amazing has happened. The whole city has come to life. There is a beautiful rosy glow as far as I can see. Everything looks warm and wonderful."

The Prince smiled slowly then said, "But I can feel you shivering, Swallow. You are cold. You must leave and join your companions before it gets any colder."

The Swallow looked up at his friend, now blind and bare. He thought for a moment.

"I think I will stay here a while longer."

Swallow was tired. He snuggled in for the night between the Prince's feet, where he soon fell asleep.

But he did not sleep for long. Shivering with cold, he awoke and looked up to see snow falling silently from the still, black sky.

Now struggling, Swallow flew onto the Prince's shoulder for the last time, and gently kissed him on the cheek. As the clock tower began to strike midnight, the little bird fell lifeless to the Prince's feet.

At the final stroke of midnight, there was a sudden cracking noise, loud enough to wake the squirrels sleeping nearby. It was the sound of the Prince's leaden heart, breaking into pieces.

The next morning there was a beautiful
carpet of glistening snow over the
Great City as the mayor and the
town clerk strutted proudly
through the park.

"Good heavens! What has happened
to the Happy Prince? He is so shabby!"
the mayor exclaimed. "Make a note to have him
hauled away. He's ruining our beautiful city! Look,
there's even a dead bird by his feet."

AND SO THE STATUE of the Happy Prince was pulled down. Workers took it to the city furnace where it was melted down so the metal could be used for something more beautiful.

However, the men at the furnace were puzzled when the broken pieces of the lead heart would not melt. "Never mind," one of them said. "Just toss them on the junk pile, along with that dead bird." And so they did.

But the good deeds of the little Swallow and the Happy Prince had not gone unnoticed.

The bird and the broken lead heart were tenderly lifted out of the junk pile, and given a place of honor.

COMPASSION

And there
they remain
to this day.

HOMELESSNESS IN AMERICA

As many as three million Americans experience homelessness over the course of a given year. The face of homelessness has changed drastically in our country over the past decades. Today, more and more working- and middle-class families face the prospect of living on the streets.

The faltering economy, skyrocketing housing prices, corporate cutbacks, and the devastating reduction in social services are forcing families out of their homes and onto the streets. The Department of Housing and Urban Development's (HUD) report "The Forgotten Americans—Homelessness: Programs and the People They Serve" revealed that some 11 million Americans are at a *high risk of homelessness*.

HELP USA offers comprehensive services for the homeless and those at risk of becoming so. In addition to providing for the immediate need of shelter, **HELP USA**'s other services include: employment training, job placement, financial assistance, child care, health care, and mentoring. It helps people in need to become self-sufficient.

Sleeping Bear Press, an imprint of Thomson Gale, is pleased to partner with **HELP USA** and contribute to their efforts on behalf of homeless people across the country as well as those at risk of homelessness.

A donation of $1.00 from the sale of each copy of *The Happy Prince* will be made to **HELP USA** to assist millions of homeless, across the country, work toward self-sufficiency! Thank you for purchasing this book. You have participated in helping someone to help themselves.

To learn more about homelessness and the work of **HELP USA**, please call 212-400-7000 or log onto www.helpusa.org.

"NO ACT OF KINDNESS, HOWEVER SMALL, IS EVER WASTED."
— *Aesop*

Although the original story of *The Happy Prince* was written over a hundred years ago, its message is as relevant today as it was when Oscar Wilde first wrote it. Opportunities abound for making a positive change in someone else's life.

Although he didn't know their names, the Happy Prince cared about those around him. You, too, don't have to personally know those you help. Many communities have local organizations that help people in need and can use your support. Here's one easy way. On your own or working with friends, create an "I Care Box" filled with toiletries, bottled water, and other items that are useful after disasters such as fires, hurricanes, or earthquakes. Decorate the box and give it to a local organization for distribution when needed.

Your words can be just as important as your deeds. Using kind, courteous words like, "May I please …" is a win-win situation. The person hearing the words wins because he feels appreciated and respected. The person saying the words wins because he feels good inside. Make a list of five kind words. Try to use all five words every day for five days.

Is it possible to make a virtue such as "caring" a habit? Founding Father Benjamin Franklin believed that being and doing good should be a lifelong endeavor. He listed 13 virtues he wanted to improve, and worked every week to develop one trait. After 13 weeks he repeated the list. He recorded his successes and failures in a journal. When Franklin was 78 he said this process made him a happier person. Follow Franklin's example by creating a "Character Journal." List one trait to improve and, for one week, discover ways to demonstrate that trait in your life. Record in your journal what you did each day to exhibit that trait.

—Michael Shoulders, EdD, educator, literacy consultant, and children's book author